PopularMMOs

PAT + JEN, the stars of PopularMMOs, are two of the most popular YouTubers in the world. With over 16.9 million subscribers and 14 billion combined views, their Minecraft-inspired channel is one of the most-watched channels on YouTube. To learn more, visit Pat and Jen on YouTube @PopularMMOs and @GamingwithJen.

To Hazel and Ezra —D.J.

A special thanks to Joe Caramagna for all his creative help!

HarperAlley is an imprint of HarperCollins Publishers.

ISBN 978-0-06-308038-6 (trade bdg.) — ISBN 978-0-06-314398-2 (special edition)

The artist used an iPad Pro and the app Procreate to create the digital illustrations for this book.
Typography by Erica De Chavez 21 22 23 24 25 PC/LSCC 10 9 8 7 6 5 4 3 2 1 ❖ First Edition

POPULARMMOS

PRESENTS

INTO THE OVERWORLD

By **PAT+JEN** from **POPULARMMOS**
Illustrated by **DANI JONES**

HARPER
alley

An imprint of HarperCollinsPublishers

Hey, what's going on, guys!

It's Pat and Jen, and we're so thrilled that you're reading our fourth book! A lot has changed since *A Hole New World* first came out. Jen's discovered that she has a sister! (Spoiler alert: it's Evil Jen!) And she's off on a new quest to unlock the deep, dark secrets about the rest of her family. It's an adventure filled with unexpected revelations, daring double crosses, and all your favorite PopularMMOs characters, from Bomby to Herobrine to Honey Boo Boo.

But most of all, what means the world to us is your continued support. Honestly, when we first started writing this series, we only had the vaguest sense of where it would all go. But the places it's taken us to and the things we've discovered along the way— it's more than we could have imagined when we started out. If you haven't read *A Hole New World*, *Enter the Mine*, or *Zombie's Day Off* yet, we highly recommend you do. They're good fun and all available now in paperback and all the craziness will mean so much more if you come along for the full ride!

Anyway, it's been a crazy adventure. Even we didn't expect the twists and turns that happen here. Have fun! Read on! We think you'll be surprised by what happens next.

And, as always, thanks for being a fan.

We love you!

Pat + Jen

PAT & JEN

Pat is an awesome dude who's always looking for an epic adventure with his partner, Super Gamer Jen. Pat loves to have fun with his friends and take control of every situation with his cool weapons and can-do attitude. Jen is the sweetest person in the world and loves to laugh, but don't let her cheeriness fool you—she's also fierce. In fact, she could be an even greater adventurer than Pat . . . if she weren't so clumsy. Even when they go on their own separate adventures they—along with their savage cat, Cloud—have a bond that can never be broken.

CARTER

Carter is Jen's best friend and her biggest fan, but he doesn't seem to like Pat very much at all. Carter is also not very smart and sometimes carries a pickle that he uses as a sword!

EVIL JEN

Evil Jen's favorite thing is chaos. She lives for wreaking havoc on the world. What makes her truly evil, however, is that she would take someone as sweet as her twin sister, Jen, and enjoy being an evil version of her.

HEROBRINE

Herobrine longs to be the king of all realms. He's as evil as evil gets, and he'll stop at nothing to get what he wants. It has been revealed recently that Herobrine is Jen and Evil Jen's father. But he also has another secret that will change everything for Pat and Jen.

HONEY BOO BOO

Honey Boo Boo is a golem of iron on the outside, but is all softy on the inside!

BOB

Bob is the former best friend of Valentine, the archer elf. He has been locked away with Valentine in Herobrine's dungeon, but Herobrine has other plans.

BOMBY

Bomby is somewhat of a pet to Pat and Jen but also Pat's best friend. He's loyal to Pat and always ready to step in for his friend when he's needed.

MR. RAINBOW

Mr. Rainbow is a magical sheep whose wool can appear to be any color of the rainbow. He has vowed to bring Jen and Evil Jen to meet their mother, but Mr. Rainbow is keeping a deep, dark secret. . . .

GIZMO

Gizmo is a magical unicorn who leaves a trail of rainbows wherever he goes. Mr. Rainbow will do anything to keep Gizmo safe.

JUMBLISFOIWTHOWEWUWUWASHESUSOSH

This Pigman is Gizmo's cellmate and an expert on healing diseases. To make it easy, let's just call him Jim.

ZOMBIE QUEEN

Jen and Evil Jen's mother is the zombie queen of the Overworld. She holds a grudge against her former partner, Herobrine, and will stop at nothing to get revenge on him!

*TO LEARN MORE ABOUT PAT & JEN'S ADVENTURES IN THE UNDERWORLD, CHECK OUT THEIR LAST BOOK, **ZOMBIE'S DAY OFF!***